THE CALL OF THE WILD

JACK LONDON

BOOKS

Editor: Leone Peguero
Cover Illustration: Terry Riley
Illustrations: Jan Scherpenhuizen
Typesetting: Midland Typesetters

The Call of the Wild
First published in 2007 by
Budget Books Pty Ltd
45–55 Fairchild Street
Heatherton Victoria 3202 Australia

10 9 8 7 6 5 4 3 2
12 11 10 09 08

ISBN: 978 1 7418 1481 1

Printed & bound in India

The Author
Jack London

American writer Jack London (1876–1916) joined the Klondike Gold Rush as a young man in 1897. That was where he learned about sled dogs and wolves, and the rugged, dangerous life on the goldfields. He used all those experiences in *The Call of the Wild*, his most famous book.

Born in San Francisco, Jack London had a remarkable career; newspaper boy, cannery laborer, sailor, hobo, university student, writer and war correspondent. His first work was published in his high school magazine. He was only 27 when *The Call of the Wild* was published in 1903. His other popular books include *White Fang* and *Sea Wolf*.

Historical note
"Gold! Gold! Gold!" cried the newspapers in 1896 after George Carmack and his two Indian companions, Skootum Jim and Dawson Charlie,

Charlie, found gold at Bonanza Creek. The Klondike Gold Rush, perhaps the greatest the world had ever seen, had begun. From all over the world, thousands of prospectors arrived at Skagway and set off on the dangerous trail north in search of their fortunes on the Klondike. Today, you can still follow the trail of Jack London's hero, Buck. The Yukon is now a major tourist area.

Contents

Introduction

Buck was Judge Wheeler's favorite pet dog. He had just been fed and was lying at his master's feet, in front of a blazing fire.

How was Buck to know that his easy life in California was about to come to a sudden and violent end?

In a few moments time, he would begin a wild, dangerous and extraordinary journey that would change his life forever.

Buck was staring into the flames, his eyes blinking shut now and again as he started to doze. Never had a dog been so happy with his lot.

Judge Wheeler was asleep in his armchair with a newspaper on his lap. The headline printed across the top of the newspaper read:

Klondike Gold Rush

It was 1897 and thousands of adventurers were hurrying to Canada's frozen Northland in search of gold on the Klondike River.

Buck didn't know that those fortune hunters would want strong dogs to pull their sleds through the snow; or that those dogs would need thick coats to survive the freezing cold.

There was something else that Buck didn't know. Manuel, Judge Miller's gardener, was a gambler. He'd lost a lot of money and needed more to pay his debts.

And Buck, with his magnificent, powerful body and thick glossy coat, was worth a fortune.

Chapter 1
Buck is Stolen

Judge Wheeler was still asleep when the gardener, Manuel, crept into the room. Buck opened a lazy eye and saw the gardener beckon to him.

Buck trusted Manuel. The gardener often took him out at night, for a walk.

With one last look at the glowing fire, the Judge's inseparable companion got up, wagged his tail and followed Manuel out of the room.

Manuel put a rope around Buck's neck and led him out of the house. No one saw them leave the house. And no one saw them arrive soon after, at the small flag station. A man was waiting there for them, in the shadows.

Manuel whispered to the man for a moment and then handed Buck over. In return, the man gave the gardener a thick roll of money.

"He's a bargain," said the man. "The dog will fetch a pile of gold up on the Klondike. Just look at that thick coat."

Buck didn't understand what was going on. When the loose end of the rope was handed to the stranger, he growled.

Buck's growl was only a warning. He had the strength of his father, a huge St. Bernard dog, and the pride of his mother, a Scottish shepherd dog.

So strangers usually paid attention to Buck's growls. This man did not. To Buck's surprise, instead the rope tightened around his neck so he could hardly breathe.

Now, Buck was really angry. In a rage, he sprang at the man. The man was ready for him and caught him by the throat with his right hand. Then, with a clever twist, he threw the dog on his back.

The rope tightened. Buck struggled in a fury, his tongue lolling out of his mouth, his great chest panting desperately for air.

Never had he been treated so cruelly. Never in his life had he been so angry.

Unable to breath, Buck fell unconscious.

He did not hear the train steaming into the station with a squeal of brakes and a shower of sparks. Nor did he hear the baggage car door being opened before he was thrown in.

***

In front of the blazing fire

Buck's next memory was of waking up and being jolted about in some kind of vehicle. The terrifying shriek of the train whistling at a road crossing finally told him where he was. He had often traveled on the railroad with the Judge and he now knew that he was in a baggage car.

He was not alone. Manuel was not to be seen, but the man who had paid the money was sitting close by.

Buck's eyes opened wide and into them came the fury of a kidnapped king. He leapt at his captor. The man grabbed the rope around Buck's neck, but the dog was too quick for him.

Buck's jaws snapped on his hand and stayed locked on it, until the man managed to choke him by twisting the rope with his other hand.

Buck slumped senseless again.

His jaws closed on the man's hand.

Chapter 2
The Lesson of the Club

Buck's journey on the train lasted several days.

During that time, he often thought of his kind master. Sometimes he would wake up in the middle of the night and imagine he saw the Judge coming towards him with a plate of hot food.

Buck was given nothing to eat or drink. He did not mind the hunger so much, but the lack of water caused him great suffering.

His eyes were bloodshot and he had become a raging fiend. Buck was so changed that even the Judge might not have recognized him.

Buck's destination was Seattle, which was at the end of the line. He was put into a wooden cage and carried by four men into a yard, which was surrounded by a high wall.

A stout man wearing a red sweater was waiting for him.

Buck realized that this man was to be his

Imagining he saw the judge

next tormentor. He hurled himself savagely against the bars of the cage.

"You're not going to try and tame him now, are you?" asked one of the men.

"Sure," said the man in the red sweater, as he opened the cage door.

The four men, who had carried in Buck's crate, scattered and perched themselves on top of the wall, from where they could watch in safety.

"Now, you red-eyed devil," said the man, picking up a heavy wooden club.

Buck's coat was bristling with anger, his mouth was foaming and there was a mad glitter in his blood-shot eyes.

He launched his huge weight straight at the man in a fury of pent up anger.

In mid-air, just as his jaws were about to close on the man, he received a shock that checked his body and brought his teeth together with an agonizing clip.

He whirled over, slamming into the ground on his back. He had never been struck by a club in his life, and did not understand what had happened. With a wild howl, he struggled to his feet and launched himself into the air again.

Again the shock came, and he was brought

A raging fiend

crushingly to the ground. This time he was aware that it was the club. But he was so mad he could not stop.

A dozen times he charged. And as often, the club broke the charge and smashed him down.

Buck slowly got to his feet. His beautiful coat was covered in blood. For the last time he rushed.

The man in the red sweater coolly gave him a terrible blow on the nose.

Buck sank to the ground, as a red mist fell across his eyes.

"That fellow is no fool when it comes to breaking dogs," cried one of the men on the wall.

"That kind of thing is not for me," said another.

He knew a thing or two about dog training and he had never seen a dog broken so cruelly.

Chapter 3
Buck's Journey North

Buck's senses returned but not his strength. He lay where he had fallen and watched the man in the red sweater.

"So your name's Buck," said the man. He was reading from a letter that had been sent along with Buck's cage. "Well, Buck my boy, we've had our little fight. Now, the best thing we can do is let it go at that."

The man seemed almost friendly. "That beating taught you your place," he said. "Be a good dog and all will go well. Be a bad dog and I'll knock the stuffing out of you, good and proper. Understand?"

As he spoke, the man patted Buck's head without fear, and Buck let him do it without growling.

When the man brought him water, he lapped up every drop. Later, he ate a big meal of raw meat, chunk by chunk, straight from the man's hand. He was beaten, he knew that. But he was not broken.

Buck saw, once and for all, that he stood no chance against a man with a club. He had learned a lesson that he would never forget.

It was his introduction to the rule of primitive law. And Buck faced these facts with all the natural cunning of his kind. He knew that he would have to change, in order to survive.

***

Buck was put in a shed overlooking the yard, with many other dogs. They each had their own small iron-barred cage.

As the days went by, other dogs arrived. Some came in quietly. Others arrived raging and snarling, as Buck had done.

One by one, Buck saw them all receive the thrashing that he had suffered at the hands of the man. The lesson was always clear. A man with a club was a lawgiver. A master to be obeyed.

Now and again, men came to buy the dogs, which were taken away.

Then came the day when a small man, who spoke English with a French accent, walked up to his cage and looked him over.

Scharpenhuizen

"Only three hundred dollars and a gift at that price."

He liked what he saw. "How much," the man cried, "for that one fine bully dog?"

"Only three hundred dollars, and a gift at that price," said the man in the red sweater. "And seeing that you are buying for the government, you can't complain."

Perrault agreed.

It was not an unfair sum for so fine an animal. It would help make sure that the Canadian government's mail was delivered quickly.

Perrault knew dogs, and saw at once that Buck was special. "One in a thousand," he said to himself.

He bought another dog too, Curly. She was a good-natured, Newfoundland hound.

That evening, Buck and Curly were loaded aboard a ship called the *Narwhal*.

It was the last time that they would see the warm Southland, and the last time Buck saw the man in the red sweater.

Chapter 4
Buck Meets Spitz

On board the *Narwhal*, Perrault and his partner, François, took the dogs below deck. There, Buck and Curly met two other dogs. One of them was a big, snow-white fellow called Spitz.

The dog seemed friendly enough, but in a treacherous sort of way. Spitz could smile at the same time as play nasty tricks on weaker dogs.

The other dog on the ship was Dave. A gloomy character, he just ate, slept and yawned a lot. He made it quite clear that there would be trouble if he wasn't left alone.

At the first meal Spitz stole Buck's food.

Before Buck could spring to punish him, François caught Spitz a stinging crack with his whip.

Buck recovered his food and looked up at François gratefully. That was very fair of him to help.

Buck had learned quickly that François and

Perrault were fair men and no fools when it came to dogs.

***

It was a rough sea voyage. The *Narwhal* bucked and rolled through the waves.

Curly was very frightened. Buck, as bold a dog as you could meet, didn't like it either. But Dave just raised his head, yawned and went back to sleep.

As the days passed, the weather was steadily growing colder.

Then one morning the dogs woke to discover that the ship had stopped. They were at the end of their journey.

It was colder than ever. They heard excited voices talking above them. François tied Buck, Spitz, Curly and Dave together with a rope and brought them up.

As Buck set foot on deck, his feet sank into a bed of freezing white stuff. He leapt back with a frightened snort. More of the white stuff was falling from the sky. It settled on his coat. Buck shook himself, but more of it fell on him.

Buck sniffed at it. Then he cautiously licked

Scherphuizen

A stinging crack with his whip

some of it. It was very cold, but it disappeared as soon as it touched his tongue.

Onlookers saw Buck's puzzled look and laughed.

Buck could not understand why everyone was laughing. How was he to know? He had never seen snow before.

Chapter 5
The Law of Club and Fang

The ship had brought the dogs to Skagway, a wild frontier seaport. Here gold prospectors loaded their sleds for the long journey north to the Klondike.

Buck's first day was a nightmare, full of shocks and surprises.

He found himself in a primitive world, very far from the civilized town that had been left behind. Here was a need for constant alert.

Both dogs and men were savages. They knew no law but the law of club and fang.

Buck had never seen dogs fight as these wolfish creatures fought. His first experience taught him a terrible lesson. Curly was the victim.

Buck and the other dogs had been taken to a camp near the town's log store. There were dozens of sleds there and many more dogs.

Curly had always been a friendly dog. She liked to sniff noses with other dogs. So she

The seaport of Skagway

Scherpenhuizen

approached a husky dog, the size of a full-grown wolf, though not half as large as she.

There was no warning.

The husky leapt and Curly's face was ripped open, from eye to jaw.

This was how wolves attacked, striking quickly with fangs and ripping the flesh as they drew back. But there was more to it than this. Thirty or forty huskies ran at once to the spot and formed a silent circle.

Buck did not understand the sudden, terrible silence. Nor did he understand the eager way the dogs were licking their lips.

Curly knew she must fight and rushed her attacker. The husky met her midway.

Curly didn't have a chance. Her opponent was far too skilful a fighter. In a moment, she had been flung on her back.

Curly was never to find her feet again.

That was the sign the other dogs had been waiting for. They closed in, snarling and yelping. Soon Curly was buried under a mass of bloodthirsty dogs.

François and Perrault rushed in to help, lashing out with their clubs and screaming at the huskies. The crazed animals did eventually run off. But Curly was already dead.

François and Perrault rush in to help.

She lay there, limp and lifeless in the blood-stained snow. She had been almost torn to pieces.

That scene often came back to haunt Buck in his sleep. So that was the way things were going to be, from now on. No fair play.

The lesson Buck learned was that once a dog was knocked off its feet, that was the end. He would see to it that he never went down.

There was something else Buck had learned from that dreadful fight. He had seen Spitz run out from the pack with blood on his tongue, and laugh.

From that moment on, Buck hated Spitz with a bitter and deep hatred.

Chapter 6
More Lessons

Before Buck had recovered from the shock of Curly's death, he received another. One morning, François fastened a number of straps and buckles on him.

It was a harness, like those put on horses at the Judge's home. It seemed that he too was to work. He helped haul François on a sled to the forest that surrounded the valley. Then they returned with a load of firewood.

Though being made a work animal upset him, he was too wise to rebel.

François was stern, demanding instant obedience. And with his whip he quickly got it.

Dave was already an experienced sled dog, so he took an important place immediately in front of the sled. He helped to steer it. His job was called the wheeler. From behind, he nipped poor Buck whenever he made a mistake.

Spitz was the leader, and also experienced.

He could not get to Buck, but growled at him to make him go in the right direction.

Buck learned easily from the other dogs and François. Before they got back to camp, he knew to stop at "Ho!" and to go ahead at "Mush!" He knew to swing wide on the bends and to keep clear of the wheeler when the loaded shed went downhill close to their heels.

"They're three very good dogs," said François to Perrault. "Buck learns quick as anything. He'll be one good dog."

Buck was starting to learn the secrets of hauling a sled.

***

That afternoon, Perrault returned with two huskies to add to their team. They were called Billee and Joe. They were brothers, but as different as night and day.

Billee was an easygoing dog. Joe was the opposite. He was a sour dog with a fixed snarl and a damaged eye.

Buck greeted the two in a companionable way. Dave simply ignored them. But Spitz made it clear he intended to thrash them both.

Billee wagged his tail to tell Spitz he would

not make trouble. But it did no good so he tried to run away. Still Spitz's sharp teeth marked his flank.

But no matter how Spitz circled, Joe whirled around on his heels. With gleaming eyes, ears laid back and fangs ready to snap shut on any dog, he looked so terrible that Spitz had to give up on disciplining him.

Spitz would have to make do with chasing Billee.

***

That evening Sol-leks arrived.

His name meant the Angry One. He was old, long and thin. He had a battle-scarred face and only one eye. He looked as if he wanted respect.

The dog team

Sol-leks was rather like Dave. He expected nothing and gave nothing. When he marched slowly into the middle of the other dogs, even Spitz left him alone.

Sol-leks could react angrily, as Buck discovered. With only his right eye, Sol-leks had a blind side. He panicked when other dogs came near him on this side. Buck was foolish enough to do that.

Sol-leks flashed around and cut Buck's shoulder to the bone with his fangs. The cut was long.

Buck had not meant to frighten him. He would avoid Sol-leks' blind side in the future.

Chapter 7
A Snowy Surprise

That night, Buck faced the problem of sleeping in the cold Northland.

He had been used to sleeping in the Judge's warm house. So he naturally entered Perrault and François's warm tent, expecting to sleep there. But they threw curses and cooking pots at him until he fled back outside, into the cold.

Buck lay down in the snow and tried to sleep. But it was too cold. He kept getting up and wandering around to keep warm.

The strange thing was that all the other dogs had vanished. He set off to find them.

With drooping tail and shivering body, Buck now looked a very sad sight indeed. He wandered aimlessly around the camp.

Suddenly, the snow gave way under his front legs and he sank down. Something was wriggling under his feet. Buck sprang back, bristling and snarling. He was frightened at what he might have found.

The sound of a friendly little yelp caught his ear, and a puff of warm air touched his nostrils. There, curled up under the snow in a snug ball, lay Billee.

Billee whined to show that he was glad he had shown Buck the secret of keeping warm at night. He even licked Buck's face with his warm, wet tongue.

Another lesson had been learned.

Buck scurried off and found a good spot. Without any fuss and effort, he dug a hole in the snow for himself and nestled in. The heat from his body filled the space and he was soon asleep. The snow hole was as warm as a kennel in sunny California.

The day had been long and hard, and he slept soundly. Though he did growl and bark, as nightmares of Curly's death filled his head.

Buck did not open his eyes until the noises of the camp woke him the next morning. At first he did not know where he was. It had snowed during the night and now he was completely buried.

Buck panicked. The greatest fear an animal could have was that of being trapped. Instinct took over. Every muscle in his body tightened. The hair on his neck and shoulders stood on

Buck dodges the cooking pots.

end. And with a ferocious snarl, he exploded out of his snow bed and into the new day.

He landed on his feet and looked up. Much to his surprise, he was still in the camp. Then he remembered how he had dug himself into the snow hole the previous night.

François saw that Buck had discovered the secret of keeping warm at night. "See, Buck learns as quick as anything," he said.

Perrault nodded in agreement. He for one was glad that he had a dog as good as Buck for the long and dangerous journey to the Klondike.

Chapter 8
Mush! Mush!

Perrault brought three more huskies to the camp. They were called Pike, Dub and Dolly. That brought the team to nine.

The dogs were harnessed soon after to the fully loaded sled. Perrault was in a hurry to leave. He had letters, parcels and goods to deliver up north.

"Mush! Mush!" François cracked the whip and the team started to pull.

Buck's first big journey had begun.

The dogs had their very own position in the traces. Sol-leks was placed in front of Buck. And Dave remained as wheeler.

Because Buck was placed between Dave and Sol-leks, they were able to teach him some tricks. And if Buck was a good learner, his teachers were sharp.

Dave's teeth were enough to remind him if he did something wrong. And Sol-leks was quick with a nip and a growl if he made the smallest of mistakes.

The rest of the team strung out ahead. At the very front was the leader, Spitz. He was the most experienced sled dog. For the moment, he was unchallenged in that position. Billie and Joe were side by side, followed by Pike, Dub and Dolly.

Once, after a short halt, Buck got his feet tangled in the traces and delayed the start. Dave nipped him sharply. Buck always kept his heels well clear of the traces after that.

Buck was glad to be on the move. Though the work was hard, he did not mind it so much. What did surprise him was how the whole team became so alive when they were working together.

Dave and Sol-leks were totally changed animals. All their lazy ways had vanished. Now they were alert and anxious to pull. They even growled when they were delayed by deep snow, or one of the other dogs was not working hard enough.

They were born to pull sleds. It seemed to be their very reason for living.

The first day's journey was a hard run up the canyon and into the high forests. As they climbed further, the forest died away as trees couldn't grow in the chilly northern lands.

Crossing glaciers and snowdrifts

They crossed glaciers and deep snowdrifts. Finally, they crossed the great Chilkoot Divide, a high mountain range. Everyone heading north had to cross it.

***

They made good time down the lakes and pulled into a camp at the head of Lake Bennett, late at night. The lake was completely frozen over and thousands of gold-seekers were camped there. As they waited for the ice to melt in the spring, they spent their time building boats. They would use them to continue their journey further north, to the goldfields.

Others, like François and Perrault, were used to winter travel by sled across ice-bound lakes and frozen rivers. They would be off in the morning.

Buck dug a hole in the snow and slept at once. He was exhausted.

Chapter 9
Survive or Die

It was as if Buck had only been asleep for a few minutes when he awoke the next day. It was freezing cold and still dark.

The dogs were quickly put into their harnesses and attached to the sled.

That day, they covered forty miles. The snow on the trail was packed hard, because many people had gone before them. So they moved fast.

The next day, they took their own track. Perrault wanted to find a short cut. The dogs had to work harder than ever to pull the sled through the fresh, deep snow.

In very deep snow, Perrault walked ahead, packing the snow with his big snowshoes to make it easier for the dogs. Later, they moved onto the river ice.

Perrault, always in a hurry, prided himself on his knowledge of ice, snow and water. He could tell where the ice was thick and, more importantly, where it was thin. Without him, they might have vanished without trace in the wilderness.

The days were long and hard. They broke camp before first light and were on the track before sunrise. It was often dark before the tents were pitched again.

Buck was always starving. The small ration of dried salmon that he was given each day seemed to go nowhere. He never had enough, and suffered from constant hunger pangs.

The other dogs seemed to manage with even less, but they weren't as big as Buck.

When Buck was with the Judge, he had plenty of time to eat his food. No other dog would dare try and steal it. Now, he found that his mates would wolf down their food and then steal what was left on his plate.

There was no defending it. While he was fighting off two or three other dogs, the food would be fast disappearing down the throats of the others. He soon put a stop to that though. He started gobbling down his food as fast as they did.

Buck watched and learned all the time.

One day he saw Pike, one of the new dogs, steal a slice of bacon when Perrault's back was

Perrault walks ahead.

turned. So Buck did the same the next day. But he went one better and got away with a whole chunk of bacon.

A great uproar followed when the bacon was discovered missing. No one suspected Buck. Dub, an awkward little fellow who was always getting caught stealing, was blamed and punished for Buck's theft.

Buck was learning to survive in the hostile North. He was changing himself to fit into his new, harsh life.

There was no time for the polite manners of his old home. In the south, there was no need to steal. Now he stole food, not for the joy of it, but because it was necessary for survival. Unless he stole, he would not have enough to eat.

Buck did not rob openly, but stole secretly and with cunning, out of respect for the rule of club and fang. Here in the icy wastes, it was a case of do what was necessary to survive, or die.

Buck's change was rapid. His muscles were now as hard as iron. He hardly felt pain any more. He also learned to eat anything that would give him energy. Stinking rotten flesh, long-dead animals; he would eat them all.

His senses of sight and sound became acute.

Singing the ancient song of his ancestors

If he heard the slightest sound in his sleep, he knew instantly whether it meant trouble or not.

He learned to nibble out the ice that formed between his toes. If he was thirsty, he could eat snow. He could break the ice too. He would rear up on his hind legs and drop down with all his weight, striking the ice with his paws.

His senses became so sharp he could sniff the air before he went to dig his sleeping hole, and tell in which direction the wind would be blowing the next morning. So he always woke snug and sheltered, with the wind at his back.

Life had been so cozy and comfortable with the Judge that Buck had lost all the instincts of his wild ancestors. Now those ancient instincts were reawakening in him.

Deep inside, Buck felt the spirits of his ancestors telling him what to do.

They showed him how they used to run as a pack in the ancient forests. They helped him to find food. They showed him how to fight like a wolf, with cut and slash and a snapping jaw.

And on still, cold nights, he pointed his nose at a star and howled like a wolf.

Buck was singing the ancient song of his ancestors.

Chapter 10
Buck and Spitz

Buck's new cunning grew. Yet it was a secret growth. Not only did he not pick fights, he deliberately avoided them. In the bitter hatred between Spitz and himself, he was patient.

On the other hand, Spitz eyed Buck suspiciously all the time. He always showed his teeth and went out of his way to bully Buck.

The showdown between them would have come sooner, except for a terrible incident.

At the end of one day they made camp beside Lake Labarge. The driving snow and wind cut like a knife.

Buck made his nest in the snow. He was so warm and snug that he hardly wanted to leave it when François called him for his food. When he returned, he found his nest occupied. A warning snarl told him that the trespasser was Spitz.

Until now Buck had avoided trouble with

his enemy, but this was too much. The beast in him roared. He leapt at Spitz.

François saw what had happened and cheered Buck on. "Give it to him! Spitz is a thief!" he shouted. "Give it to him!"

Spitz was equally willing. He circled back and forth, waiting for his chance to spring. Buck did the same.

It was then that the unexpected happened. It was the event that was to put off their fight for some considerable time.

A warning from Perrault gave the alert. "Dogs! A whole pack of them."

Buck turned and saw in the dim light that a pack of starving huskies had crept in while Buck and Spitz had prepared to fight. There must have been a hundred of them. They were crazed by the smell of food, having scented the camp from an Indian village.

In an instant, the beasts were tearing at the food stores. François and Perrault attacked them with clubs. They yelped and howled, but still kept eating.

The astonished sled dogs burst out of their nests. The fierce invaders set upon them.

Buck had never seen such dogs. They were mere skeletons. Yet, their hunger-madness

"Give it to him! Spitz is a thief!"

made them terrifying. There was no stopping them.

Buck was attacked by three of them. They slashed and ripped at his head and shoulders. Billee was howling in fear. Dave and Sol-leks, soon dripping blood from several wounds, were fighting bravely side by side.

Joe was snapping like a demon. He finally clamped his teeth around the leg of one husky and bit him to the bone. At that, the normally lazy Pike leapt on the crippled animal and broke its neck with a flash of his teeth.

Buck took one of the invaders by the throat. Then he felt a set of teeth sink into his side. He turned and saw that it was not one of the starving huskies. It was Spitz.

Spitz's attack was pure cunning. He wanted the starving huskies to kill Buck for him. All he had to do was put Buck on his back. The huskies would come in for the kill.

Buck knew that too. He snarled and bared his teeth. He fought desperately to stay on his feet and, at last, shook himself free.

Buck took one hateful look at Spitz before running off to join the other dogs.

Chapter 11
Buck's New Boots

All nine dogs survived the attack by the starving huskies, but every one of them was wounded.

Dub was badly injured on the hind leg. Dolly had a ripped throat. Joe had lost an eye and Billee had his ear chewed to ribbons. He cried and whimpered all day.

Buck saw Spitz join them later. He snarled at him.

François and Perrault discovered that the crazed animals had taken most of the food, and they had chewed through the sled ropes, the leather whip and the canvas coverings.

Perrault was very angry. With a 400-mile trail still between him and Dawson City, the last thing he wanted was trouble like this. It would mean another delay.

***

Two hours of cursing and mending saw the

wounded team back on the trail. They were now on the most difficult part of the track. It was called the Thirty Mile River.

Even the coldest frost had not been able to freeze up this river completely. The water was still flowing in the middle. The ice was just about thick enough to travel on along the banks. But it was terribly thin in places.

The first near disaster happened when Perrault, leading the team on foot, suddenly fell through the ice.

The pole he was carrying saved him. It got caught above the hole in the ice. Perrault was left hanging. François crawled over to him and hauled him up.

Perrault fell though the icy trail many times. And after each freezing bath in the river, François lit a fire to warm him up and dry his clothes.

Once, Buck and Dave fell through the ice. They were half-frozen and all but drowned by the time they were dragged out.

Again, the men lit a fire to warm them.

Later, Spitz fell through and took with him the whole team except Buck. Buck had to use all his strength to stop them being washed away downstream.

Perrault falls through the ice.

They covered less than a quarter-mile that day.

By the time they made camp, Buck and the rest of the team were exhausted.

The next part of the trail was easier.

They covered thirty-five miles the following day and reached the Big Salmon River. The day after, they covered another thirty-five miles to the Little Salmon. On the third day, it was forty miles and they reached Five Finger Rapids.

Buck's feet were starting to trouble him. He had never gone so far in his life before. He had never needed tough paws at the Judge's place. Now they were covered in blisters and cut to pieces on the ice and rocks. He was limping badly.

Perrault rubbed Buck's feet for half an hour after supper. Later, he cut up his own moccasins and sewed them into four small boots for the dog.

That gave Buck great relief, and brought a smile to Perrault's face.

One morning, Perrault found Buck on his back with his four legs waving in the air. He realized that Buck was waiting for him to put on his dog moccasins!

There was no way that Buck was going to move without his boots.

Buck's New Boots

Buck's boots give him great relief.

Chapter 12
Two Devils Buck

The journey was exhausting. Still Buck and Spitz had the energy to growl and snarl at each other. There was only room for one leader. Buck now knew he would have to fight Spitz for that title.

"Spitz sure is one devil," said Perrault. "Some day he'll kill Buck."

François disagreed. "Buck is two devils! All the time I watch him and I know for sure. Listen to me. Some fine day, he'll get real mad and he'll chew up Spitz and spit him out on the snow."

Maybe Spitz did cheat and attack Buck when he wasn't looking. But Spitz was the leader dog. All his ancient instincts told him to fight Buck.

And Buck did seem very strange to Spitz. He had seen many dogs from the south. They dropped dead of too much work, or died of cold and starvation.

"Buck is two devils!"

But Buck was different. He could endure any weather conditions. And his strength matched that of a husky. Buck was also learning the savagery and cunning of the husky. He wanted that final fight for the leader's position. He wanted it because of his pride.

Things got worse when Buck started to threaten Spitz's leadership.

If Spitz tried to punish a dog, Buck would step between them. He did it deliberately, so Spitz would know the challenge was on.

One morning Pike went missing. Spitz was furious that the dog was delaying the journey. He raged through the camp, sniffing and digging in every likely spot.

Spitz found him eventually and was about to punish him when Buck leapt between them. The move surprised Spitz so much that he skidded and did a somersault.

With Spitz still trying to get to his feet, Pike saw his chance and sprang on top of the leader. So did Buck. Who knows what might have happened if they had been left alone. But François spotted them. He had had enough of the dogs fighting. He took his whip to the two attackers. Pike ran off but Buck refused to let go of Spitz. So François grabbed his club and

Buck is given a ferocious blow.

gave Buck a ferocious blow. It knocked him sideways.

Spitz got up, shook himself and set off after Pike. The lazy dog certainly got a good thrashing from his leader that day.

Buck challenged Spitz whenever he could. This had an effect on the other sled dogs.

When they knew who their leader was, they always obeyed. Now they weren't quite sure whether it was Spitz or Buck. So they weren't really working as a team any longer. There were fights going on and the dogs were getting on each other's nerves.

François knew that Spitz and Buck were the problem. He understood dogs. He knew this was a life-and-death struggle between the two. He also understood that sooner or later they would meet for the final battle.

But, for now, Dawson City was just over the next hill.

Chapter 13
Dawson City

"Ho! Ho!" François called the dogs to a halt as they pulled into Dawson City with the great fight still to come.

It was the main town for the gold hunters, but even so, it could be a lonely place for some. Many had left their families behind. That's why they were so happy to see Perrault and François arrive. The sled carried mail from their loved ones.

Buck saw that most of the dogs up here were the wild, wolf, husky breed. They were wolf mixed with husky blood. Every night, they started their nocturnal song.

It was an eerie chant. It was an old song, as old as the world's first dogs. It sounded like wailing, howling and half-sobbing. Buck joined in. He knew it was a song that his forefathers had sung. It told of fear of the night, cold, pain and hunger.

The fact that Buck understood that song was

a sign that he was leaving his past behind him. He was starting to feel the stir of his ancestors. His journey back to the wild was beginning.

In Dawson, Perrault delivered all the letters, packages and goods he had brought up. Then, he loaded up for the southbound journey.

The team spent seven days in Dawson. It helped the dogs recover from the journey there. Perrault decided that Buck did not need to wear his moccasin boots any more. His paws had hardened.

So, they set off south again. This time it was Perrault's pride, which set the pace. He wanted to make this the fastest-ever trip from Dawson to Skagway.

It was possible. The trail they had travelled up on was now packed hard from all the others who had followed behind them. The police had organized for food stores to be laid down at marked places on the track, too.

The first day they covered fifty miles. The second day saw them racing down the Yukon River.

But Buck and Spitz were still challenging each other for the leadership. And the other dogs were causing trouble. They could see that Spitz wasn't quite the leader he had been. They

The town of Dawson City

thought that perhaps Buck's time was coming.

Pike even stole half a fish from Spitz one night – but only under the protection of Buck. The dogs saw that Buck could protect them from Spitz's attacks.

Even the good-natured dogs were snarling and fighting with one another.

Perrault was furious. He stamped the snow in rage. How could he make a record run now?

François made his whip sing and crack through the air. It didn't help. As soon as his back was turned, the dogs were fighting again.

But these fights were just small.

There was only one battle that really mattered.

Chapter 14
The Battle Begins

The events which led to the final fight between Buck and Spitz started at a camp on the Takhini River.

It was evening and everyone had just finished supper. Suddenly, one of the dogs spotted a rabbit. It bolted for cover. The dogs gave chase.

The rising moon saw it all. The rabbit sped off downriver and turned off into a small creek. It was frozen over and covered with snow.

The whole dog team was in pursuit.

Some fifty other dogs that belonged to the police, who were camped nearby, joined them when they heard the excitement.

Buck led the pack, sixty strong, around bend after bend, but could get no closer to the rabbit.

The smell of the kill was in Buck's nose. He howled the old wolf-cry. Buck was never as alive as this before.

As he raced away, he did not notice the

Buck leads the pack as they chase a rabbit.

calculating Spitz leave the pack and cut across a narrow neck of land. The pack would have to take the long way round by the frozen river trail. If Spitz was right, his route was shorter.

Buck raced on. The rabbit was still ahead. Then Buck saw him. Spitz burst out of the undergrowth a short distance in front of the rabbit. It was running too fast to escape. It leapt straight into Spitz's waiting jaws.

Spitz's teeth broke its back and it wheeled into the air, shrieking out aloud. The rabbit was dead before it hit the ground.

The pack howled in delight and slowed. But not Buck. He drove on at full speed and barged straight into his enemy. Spitz and Buck tumbled to the ground.

Spitz got to his feet first and struck. He slashed Buck across the shoulder and jumped clear again. Twice, Buck's teeth clipped shut like the jaws of a steel trap. He slashed and backed away. Twice he missed his bite. His lips writhed and snarled.

Buck knew that this fight was to the death.

The two dogs circled each other, snarling, ears laid back, watching and waiting for an advantage. The other dogs were waiting too, and circled the fighters.

The Battle Begins

Buck and Spitz were silent, eyes gleaming and breath steaming in the icy air.

To Buck, it was as if he had been here before. There was nothing new or strange about this fight. He was born for this. This was the fight of his life.

Spitz was a born fighter too. He had defeated and killed all sorts of dogs. He could show bitter rage. But he never let that blind his cunning. He was a masterful foe.

He never charged until he was ready to receive a charge from and defend an attack.

Chapter 15
The Final Battle

Buck closed in again, trying to sink his teeth into Spitz's neck. Spitz was too quick. Their jaws met. Fang clashed against fang.

Buck was having trouble getting through his enemy's defenses. Time and time again, he tried for the throat. Each time Spitz slashed him away.

Now Buck tried to bluff his enemy. He pretended to be aiming for the throat again. Instead, he veered about and struck Spitz on the shoulder. He wanted to use his strength like a ram to overthrow Spitz.

Again, Spitz darted away and clawed him as he did so.

Both dogs were now covered with blood.

Buck was panting hard. He was running short of breath. Spitz saw it and made a series of charges. Buck staggered, desperate to find his footing after each attack.

At one time, the whole circle of sixty dogs

Buck strikes Spitz on the shoulder.

rose and howled out aloud. They were sure Buck had been tipped over. But, he was still up. They all sat down again and waited.

Spitz was fighting well, but Buck fought with both instinct and cunning. He rushed in again. At the last moment, he dropped his head and his teeth snapped shut on Spitz's front left leg.

There was a crunch of breaking bone. Spitz howled in agony. He still refused to go down. He stood on three legs and glared at Buck. Three times Buck tried to knock him over.

Despite his pain, Spitz struggled to stay on his feet. Then Buck repeated his trick. This time he went for the right front leg. His jaw clamped shut. Teeth met bone.

Spitz saw the silent circle, the gleaming eyes and lolling tongues. He saw the mass of dogs closing in on him. He had seen this before when he had beaten other dogs.

Only this time, he was beaten.

There was no hope for him now. There was to be no mercy. Buck moved around to make the final rush. The circle closed in.

Spitz could feel the breaths of the huskies around him. He saw that they were half crouching, ready to spring. They were waiting for him to make the final move. Every eye was fixed on him.

It was as if each animal had turned to stone. Only Spitz quivered and bristled as he staggered back and forth, roaring. He was snarling at his own coming death.

Then Buck sprang. They met shoulder to shoulder. The strike was good.

Buck stepped back as Spitz finally tumbled to the ground. The other dogs moved in for the kill. It was over quickly.

Buck looked on. He could feel his ancestors watching. He was the leader now. He had made his kill. The leadership was his prize.

Chapter 16
A New Leader

"See, Buck is two devils," said François the next day, when he discovered Spitz was missing and saw Buck covered in wounds.

"Spitz must have fought very hard," answered Perrault, looking at the cuts and fang marks all over Buck's body.

"No more Spitz. No more trouble, for sure," said François.

Perrault loaded the sled that day and François harnessed the dogs. Buck trotted up, ready to take Spitz's position as leader. That's when François made a mistake. He led Sol-leks to that place. He thought that Sol-leks was the best leader after Spitz, and that Buck was too inexperienced to take the job.

Buck snapped at Sol-leks, driving him back down the line of dogs and placing himself between the traces in the leader's position.

"Look at Buck," said François. "He's killed Spitz and thinks he can be leader."

"He thinks he can be leader."

François went up to Buck and grabbed him by the scruff of his neck. "Come here, Buck," he said, "this is not your place yet."

Buck growled. But he allowed himself to be led back down the line. François collected Sol-leks. He was about to lead him to the front again when he noticed Buck. The dog had sneaked around and taken his place at the front again.

François was getting angry. "I'll fix you, Buck," he raged, grabbing his club.

Buck remembered the man in the red sweater and moved back. He snarled as he circled François, making sure he was just out of reach of the club. No club would ever hit him again.

Each time François came him to take his old position, Buck fell back.

Buck was in open revolt. He wanted the leadership. It was his by right. He had earned it and he would not be content with anything less.

Perrault came to help François. They chased after Buck for an hour. They threw clubs at him. He dodged them all. They cursed him.

Buck answered their curses with snarls. He did not try to run away. He just kept a few paces ahead of them as they chased him around the camp. Buck made it quite clear that he would only come to them when he had got what he wanted.

François sat down and scratched his head. Perrault, who was in a hurry as usual, was angry. They should have been on the trail an hour ago.

Then François grinned sheepishly at Perrault. Both men knew they were beaten.

François led Sol-leks to his old position.

Now there was no place for Buck to go to except the front, in the leader's place. Once more François, who was still carrying his club, called him, and once more Buck refused to come.

"Throw down your club," said Perrault. "See what he does then."

François threw away his club and looked at Buck.

Buck trotted boldly up to the front of the team. He looked at each dog and then took his position as leader. François put the harness on him.

He bellowed loudly, "Mush! Mush!"

Buck's great muscles heaved. The sled moved. Gradually, the whole team pulled as one.

"Mush! Mush!" François called again.

The powerful team was now racing away down the hill towards the river.

Buck held his head high as the sled sped south once more.

Racing toward the river

Chapter 17
Buck's the Best

Buck quickly showed both François and Perrault that he was a born leader. He was quick thinking and had good judgment.

Dave and Sol-leks did not mind the change in leadership. It was none of their business, anyway. Their job was to work and pull. So long as they were left to do that, they did not care who led them.

Several of the other dogs had become unruly while the battle for the leadership was going on. Now, they buckled down and Buck quickly nipped them back into shape.

That night in camp Joe, who never stopped complaining or snarling about one thing or another, was shown how he must behave in future.

Even Spitz had never given him a beating. However Buck gave him a good thrashing and he never moaned again. And Buck's snarls quickly changed Pike's lazy ways, too.

The dogs were now working as a team again, pulling together, moving as one. Further down the track, two more huskies, Teek and Koona joined the team. Buck quickly taught them who was boss.

"I've never known a dog like Buck," said François. "He's worth a thousand dollars. What do you say, Perrault?"

Perrault nodded. "Buck's the best."

Perrault was happy now. They were making quick progress. The trail was hard. No new snow had fallen and the journey was easy. Perhaps they could make a record run after all.

All the rivers were covered with thick ice. There was no chance of falling through this time. In one day alone they covered ten times the usual distance.

Buck and his mates were heroes!

On another day, they made a sixty-mile dash from the foot of Lake Labarge to White Horse Rapids and on to Bennett.

Exactly fourteen days out, they topped the White Pass and looked down on Skagway again. It was a record run. They had averaged forty miles a day. No team had ever done it faster.

People came out into the main street to welcome the team. Buck and his mates were heroes!

Soon after arriving, François came up to Buck and put his arms around him. There were tears in the man's eyes. He was strict with his dogs but he could love them too.

He and Perrault had received new orders. They would not be on the north run any more. François had come to say farewell to the best dog he had ever known.

Saying farewell

Chapter 18
Another World

Buck and the team were sold to the Salt Water Mail. The company ran a dozen teams of dogs delivering mail from Skagway to Dawson. A Scotsman was the new owner.

Buck did not like the new work, although he always did a good job. It was boring – the same trail, the same destination. Nothing gave the team excitement any more. One day was very much like another.

There were battles between the other dog teams. Some dared to challenge Buck for his leader's position. But they were no match for him. Buck defeated all those brave enough to fight him.

The fiercest dogs now saw him as the true leader. While other dogs were allowed to be leader of their own sled, Buck always led the way when they left camp.

At night, Buck's position was nearest the campfire. That was his by right. He lay with his hind legs crouched beneath him and his forelegs stretched out in front. His head was usually raised, his eyes blinking lazily at the flames.

He was no longer homesick. The Judge's house had become a dim and distant memory. More important to Buck now was a strange instinct that kept coming back to him.

It was when he was out on the trail and had to face new problems that he felt it most. No problem was too difficult for him. He knew that someone had already taught him how to solve those problems.

Sometimes, as he sat peering into the camp-fire flames, Buck saw a man. He was almost naked and carrying an ancient axe. At other times when Buck saw this man in the flames, he was squatting by a campfire. His elbows were on his knees and his head was in his hands.

Sometimes, Buck saw the man at the same time as hearing huge monsters, crashing about in the undergrowth. He saw their eyes gleaming.

These sights and sounds were visions from another, earlier world. They frightened Buck. His neck hair would stand on end. He would start to whimper or growl. His mates thought he was dreaming.

Then he would return to his own world when the Scottish man called out: "Hey, you Buck, wake up!"

The real world returned. Buck got up, yawned and stretched as though he had been asleep all the time.

But Buck was sure the other world he had seen was real in a different, mysterious way.

Visions from an earlier world

Chapter 19
A Sad Death

None of the dogs enjoyed the regular runs from Skagway to Dawson City anymore. They had become very tired. Billee cried and whimpered in his sleep. Worse still, Dave seemed to be very ill. If the sled jerked to a halt, he cried out in pain.

Dave would creep away, make a nest and go to sleep as soon as they made camp. He only woke to eat and then slept until it was time to put on the harness in the morning.

The drivers looked at him closely. They could find nothing wrong. He cried out when they pressed him in certain places. But he had no broken bones.

On one trip, he became so weak that he kept falling down. He was dragged along until the Scotsman saw what had happened. They decided to rest him for a while, and then let him run behind. Sol-leks took his place.

Dave whimpered. He didn't like another

Dave is dragged along

dog taking his place. He was a proud dog. He was dying, yet he could not bear the thought of another dog doing his work.

One morning, the drivers found him standing inside the traces of the sled. It was the place where he had always been in the team.

Now he was begging with his eyes to be allowed to stay there and do his work.

The drivers had heard of old dogs that had clung to the sled until the very last moment of their lives. So they decided that the kindest thing to do was to leave Dave in his old position. He was harnessed and the sled set off.

Dave was so proud, as he started to pull again. The pain must have been awful because he often cried out. Sometimes he tripped in the traces and was once more dragged along by the others.

Dave held out until the next camp. Then the men made a place for him by the fire.

In the morning, he was too weak to travel. When the others were put into their harnesses, Dave crawled towards the sled. He got on his feet, staggered and fell. Then he was up again, pushing his front legs forward and dragging his hind legs behind him. Bit by painful bit, he moved towards the sled. His strength was gone.

A Sad Death

The driver walks back to the camp.

The sled left without him. They turned a bend and finally Dave could be seen no more. But Buck could now hear him howling.

The driver stopped the sled and walked back to the camp. A single yelp was heard and then, Dave made no more noise. The man hurried back to the sled, looking upset. The whips cracked and the team moved off again.

Somehow, Buck and every other dog knew what had happened.

Chapter 20
Charles, Hal and Mercedes

Working for the Salt Water Mail was exhausting work. Most of the dogs were in a terrible state. Buck lost almost a quarter of his body weight. The other dogs lost even more weight than he did.

The lazy Pike had often pretended to be lame. Now he really was. Sol-leks was limping, too. Dub had hurt his shoulder blade. They were all footsore and dead tired.

It hadn't happened overnight. The tiredness was due to months and months of work with little time to rest.

The dogs could barely keep the traces tight as they pulled. They were on their last legs when they pulled into Skagway after their latest journey.

"Mush! Mush! My sore-footed mates," cried the driver, as they rode down Skagway's main street. "This is the last trail. You'll get a long rest now. That's for sure."

The drivers truly did expect a long rest in Skagway. But it wasn't to be. The population on the Klondike was doubling every few weeks. Mountains of mail and supplies were always waiting in Skagway to be sent north. There were never enough dog teams to do the job.

The job was a tiring one for the drivers too. The Scotsman had had enough of it. One day, he came to see the dogs with two men called Charles and Hal.

Charles was a skinny middle-aged man who looked as though he wouldn't have the strength to lift a bucket of water. He had a moustache, which he twiddled with all the time.

Hal was a boastful youngster of maybe nineteen or twenty. He had a big Colt revolver and huge hunting knife strapped to a belt that bristled with cartridges. It was only to convince people he was a big and brave man.

Once more, Buck saw money exchange hands. He knew what that meant. He and the team had new owners.

It was clear that Charles and Hal were totally out of place in Skagway.

When Buck's team was taken to their new owner's camp, it was in a terrible mess. The tent

Charles and Hal

flapped in the wind. And there were unwashed dishes everywhere.

There was woman living with the two men. Her name was Mercedes. She turned out to be the wife of Charles and the sister of Hal.

The next day they started loading their sled. When the men put a sack of goods on the front of the sled, Mercedes said it should go on the back. When they put it on the back, she said it

The Sled is overloaded.

should go on the front. They argued all the time.

Everything was chaos. When they finished packing, the load towered over the sled.

People from a nearby tent came to watch what was going on. They could not help laughing.

"It's not for me to tell you your business," said one to Mercedes. "But you won't need that tent."

"How in the world could I manage without a tent?" replied Mercedes.

"It's springtime up there," said the man. "You won't need it."

The woman shook her head. She found it hard to imagine living outside without a tent. Perhaps there was a hotel, she said.

"There ain't no hotels yet," said Hal, putting the last few bits and pieces on top of the huge load. "Do you think the sled will pull this without falling over?"

"Course it will," said Charles. "Why shouldn't it?"

"I think it might be a bit top heavy," warned one of the onlookers.

"The dogs will pull that all day without any trouble," said Charles.

He intended to make them, never mind the truth of the matter.

Chapter 21
An Accident

"Mush! Mush!" Hal called on the dogs to move.

The dogs heaved. Nothing moved. They kept pulling for a few more moments and then gave up. They slumped to the ground. The sled wouldn't shift the smallest bit.

"The lazy brutes, I'll show 'em," said Hal, taking out his whip.

"Oh Hal, you mustn't," said Mercedes, wrenching the whip from his hand. "The poor dears. Now you must promise you won't be cruel to the dogs. Or I won't go one more step with you."

"Precious little you know about dogs," Hal sneered. "They're just lazy. You've got to take the whip to 'em. Those men will tell you."

Mercedes looked to the crowd, which was growing bigger all the time. "If you want to know," said one, "your dogs are just plum tuckered out. That's what the matter is. They need a rest."

An Accident

"You must promise you won't be cruel."

Hal cracked the whip above the dogs' heads. The dogs got up and dug their feet into the packed snow. They heaved with every bit of strength left in them. The sled still would not move.

The whip cracked again. The sled was going nowhere.

Mercedes dropped to her knees in front of Buck. She put her arms around him. "You poor dear, why don't you pull?" she begged. "Hal wouldn't whip you if you pulled hard."

Again, one of the onlookers tried to help. He said it would be easier if they freed the runners beneath the sled first. They were frozen to the ground.

Charles and Hal climbed onto the sled and rocked it. The sled cracked free from the ice at last.

"Mush!" cried Hal again. Slowly, very slowly, the sled started to move down the track out of town. Buck and his mates struggled under Hal's cracking whip.

A hundred yards ahead, the path turned and sloped steeply. It would have needed a more experienced man than Hal to save the day.

As they turned that corner, the top-heavy sled turned over. The load spilled out across the street. Buck broke into a run. The other dogs followed his lead.

"Whoa! Whoa!" cried Hal, before being tripped up by one of the traces. He tumbled to the ground.

Buck and his mates raced off down the street with the empty sled tumbling along behind them. The onlookers roared with laughter.

At last, a kindhearted man caught the dogs and brought them back. "If you ever expect to get to Dawson," the man told Charles and Hal, "take half the load and twice the dogs."

Charles, Hal and Mercedes didn't want to take advice. They thought they knew everything. But they got rid of the tinned food. That was very heavy.

One of the onlookers laughed again. "That canned food is the most valuable item on board," he said. "You'll need that."

The man listed the things they could leave. "You won't need blankets," he said. "Throw away the tent. Get rid of them clothes. Good Lord, anyone would think you're on a luxury express train."

Mercedes cried when her bags were thrown aside. She swore she would not travel a step without her fine clothes, but Charles and Hal insisted.

"Right!" she said, angrily. "We'll see what else can be left behind."

She stormed over to the men's things. She went through them like a tornado, throwing aside just about everything Charles and Hal owned.

At the end of it all, the sled load was a little lighter. And that evening Charles and Hal bought six more dogs. That made fourteen in all.

The new dogs were hopeless. Buck could see that. Hal drove them around the town to see how they worked together. It was clear the dogs had no idea about sled work. Buck tried to teach them, but none of the dogs had any spirit at all.

Charles and Hal were very pleased though. They had seen lots of sleds come and go in Skagway, but none had fourteen dogs. They felt very superior.

But they had forgotten one thing. A sled could never carry a load as well as enough food for fourteen dogs. Yet, Hal had worked it out exactly – so many days to cover the distance, so many pounds of dog food. It was quite simple, he thought.

This was going to be the worst journey of Buck's life.

Chapter 22
Walking Skeletons

The next morning, Buck led the longest team of dogs ever seen in Skagway down the main street.

The town folk had never seen such a sight and laughed them out of town. There was nothing cheerful about the team though. Buck and his mates were still dead weary and the new dogs were weak creatures.

Buck had journeyed to Dawson City and back four times. Now he was facing the same old trail again.

The dogs knew that they could not expect any help from their new owners. They knew nothing about driving a sled. As the days went by, it became clear that they would never learn to drive a sled either.

They had no discipline. It took them half the night to set up camp and half the morning to pack everything up again. They never did learn how to load a sled. Most of the day was spent stopping to pick up things that had fallen off.

Some days they drove less than ten miles. The journey was going to take longer than expected. The dog food was running out. Hal did another of his calculations. He doubled the dogs' food rations. He was sure they would now go twice the distance each day.

Later, Hal woke one morning and realized that half the dog food had gone, yet only a quarter of the journey had been covered. This time he cut back the rations by half. He reckoned this would double the time the food would last.

A few days later, Mercedes realized the dogs were starving. When the men weren't looking, she stole some fish to give the dogs. The truth was that it wasn't really food that the dogs needed. They needed rest.

The first to go was Dub. He was a poor blundering thief, but he had worked hard at times. He couldn't walk another yard. Hal left him behind, and that was the end of him.

Most of the new dogs just died of starvation and exhaustion soon after. The journey was simply too much for them.

Charles, Hal and Mercedes continued to quarrel amongst themselves. Sometimes Mercedes took the side of her husband, sometimes that of her brother. The result was an endless family feud.

Mercedes finally lost interest in the dogs' health. She used to walk beside the sled. Now, she rode on the sled all day. She weighed one hundred and twenty pounds. She rode on that sled until some of the exhausted dogs collapsed under the extra load.

Once, Charles and Hal forced her off the sled. She sat down in the snow like a spoilt child and refused to move.

"I will not walk another step!" she insisted.

"I will not walk another step!"

An explosion of new life

So the men gave in and let her ride on the sled again.

The dog food finally ran out at Five Finger Rapids. A toothless old trader, who lived there, swapped a few pounds of frozen meat for Hal's Colt revolver.

Through all of this, Buck staggered along at the head of the team. It was a nightmare. He pulled when he could, but he was so exhausted. He often fell down and remained there until the whip drove him to his feet again.

His beautiful coat was thin and matted with mud and blood. His muscles had wasted away to knotty strings. His ribs were almost fleshless.

Buck and his mates were walking skeletons.

It was heartbreaking to see. Yet Buck's heart was unbreakable. The man in the red sweater had proved that.

The walking skeletons moved on. There were seven of them now. They were so exhausted they didn't even feel Hal's whip any more. They were barely alive.

When the humans called a halt, the dogs dropped to the ground as if they were dead.

Billee was the next to go. The good-natured dog just fell down and couldn't get up again. Hal had sold his gun, so he clubbed Billee with the back of his ax. Billee was thrown onto the side of the track.

All the surviving dogs knew they might be the next to go. Koona died the following day. Now just five of the team survived. Joe was almost gone. Pike, crippled and limping.

The one-eyed Sol-leks was pulling with the last of his strength. Teek was the strongest because he had worked the least that year.

Finally, there was Buck. He was so weak he was only a leader in name. He could no longer feel his feet.

It was beautiful spring weather now, though neither the dogs nor humans were aware of it. Each day the sun rose earlier and set later. The whole day was a blaze of sunshine.

An explosion of new life had replaced the ghostly silence of winter.

The willow and aspen trees were bursting into life. Crickets sang at night. The birds chirped by day. Squirrels chattered in the wood. The ice was melting everywhere. Fresh streams flowed down from the mountains.

High above, the wildfowl chased the sun.

Far beneath them, two men and a woman and five exhausted huskies staggered into John Thornton's camp.

Chapter 23
Tragedy

John Thornton was a gold prospector, a kindly fellow. He had been holed up in his camp since midwinter when his feet had been badly bitten by frost. So his pals had left him there with his dogs, Skeet and Flash, to get better. They had gone on ahead to build a raft.

The plan was that they would return and, together, they would raft the final stretch to Dawson City. Thornton was carving an ax handle when Buck and the team pulled in.

Thornton didn't need to look very carefully to see what sort of people Charles, Hal and Mercedes were. The condition of the dogs and the way the sled was loaded told him everything.

He also knew that only crazy fools went by sled along the river at this time of year. Each day the ice was melting and getting thinner.

"They say the trail above here is dangerous because the ice is so thin now," said Hal. "They say we should stay here for a while."

Carving an axe handle

"They told you true," said Thornton.

"But we made it here," said Hal proudly. "We didn't need luck. The ice was strong enough to hold us."

"Only fools could have made it with a sled this far," said Thornton. "I'll tell you straight. I wouldn't risk my carcass by driving on that ice ahead, not for all the gold in the Klondike."

Hal wouldn't listen. "Rubbish. We'll show you. We'll be in Dawson before we know it."

The next morning Hal raised his whip and called on the dogs to move. "Get up there, Buck! Mush! Mush!"

Buck's head hung low. He couldn't move.

Thornton carried on carving his axe handle.

Now the whip cracked. Sol-leks was the first to struggle to his feet. Teek followed. Joe came next, yelping with pain. Pike did his best. Twice he fell over. He made it on his third attempt.

Buck made no effort at all. He just lay where he had fallen. The lash of the whip bit into him. He neither whined nor moaned.

It was too much for Thornton. There were tears in his eyes as the whipping continued.

Hal gave up with the whip and took out his club instead. Buck still refused to move. Like his mates, he was barely able to get up. But, unlike them, he had made up his mind never to pull for Hal again.

All Buck's instincts had told him that the ice beneath him on the trail was getting thinner every day. It seemed that he sensed disaster close at hand. It was waiting for them out there on the ice where his master was trying to drive him. He refused to stir.

Buck had suffered so much. He could not feel the blows from Hal's club now. The spark of life was leaving him. Buck felt strangely numb. It was as if he was aware he was being beaten, but he was seeing it all from outside his body. He was a long way away.

And then suddenly, without warning, Thornton stumbled to his feet. He was in great pain but he managed to throw himself at Hal. He butted the cruel young man in the face. Hal staggered back as though struck by a falling tree. Mercedes screamed. Charles did not get up because of his stiffness.

Thornton now stood defending Buck. He was so angry. "If you strike that dog again, I'll kill you," he roared.

"It's my dog," said Hal, wiping blood from the edge of his mouth. "Get out of my way, or I'll fix you! We are going to Dawson. And right now!"

Thornton remained standing between Buck and Hal, who now pulled out his hunting knife. Hal was no match for Thornton, who just smashed Hal's knuckles with his ax handle. The knife fell to the ground. Mercedes screamed again.

Thornton picked up the knife and cut Buck free from the traces.

Hal had no fight left him now. He called to Charles and Mercedes and said they were leaving. Soon after, the sled pulled away down the hill.

Buck was still unable to get up, but his eyes followed his mates.

Pike was leading with Sol-leks behind him. Between them were Joe and Teek. They were limping and staggering.

Mercedes was riding the sled as usual. Hal was driving and Charles stumbled along in the rear.

As Buck watched them go, Thornton knelt down beside him. His kindly hands searched for any broken bones. Fortunately, there were only bruises.

By now, the sled was almost a quarter of a mile away. Buck and Thornton watched it sliding slowly down the icy river track.

Suddenly, the sled dropped through the ice.

"Get out of my way!"

Hal was thrown into the air. They heard Mercedes scream and saw Charles turn and start to run back.

It was too late. A great slab of river ice had given way. Dogs and humans disappeared. A great, yawning hole was all that was left to be seen.

It was what the onlookers had warned about in Skagway. They said the bottom might fall out of the trail. Now it had.

Thornton and Buck looked at each other. "You poor devil," said Thornton, and Buck licked his hand.

Tragedy

Scherpenkuizen

The ice gives way.

Chapter 24
The Call of the Wild

Buck had been close to death when Thornton rescued him, and Thornton had been close to losing his toes to frostbite. Together, they slowly recovered.

They lay on the riverbank, watching the clear waters run, waiting for Thornton's friends to return with the raft.

Buck got stronger every day. He had flesh on his bones again.

He had also made friends with Thornton's dogs. Skeet was a beautiful Irish Setter. When Buck was very sick, she had licked his wounds and looked after him. Each morning, she would play the nurse.

Flash was just as friendly. He was a huge dog. He had eyes that laughed.

To Buck's surprise, Skeet and Flash were not jealous about him coming into their master's camp. They were not wild dogs. They were as kind to Buck as their master was.

Watching the clear waters

Buck realized that the love Thornton showed him was different to the affection he had received at the Judge's house in the old days.

With the Judge, it had been a dignified friendship. The Judge would pat him now and again and make sure he was well fed. That was all.

What Buck had now was real love. Thornton looked on his dogs as if they were his children. He loved them all.

Thornton had an affectionate way of taking Buck's head in his hands and placing his chin on the top of his head. Then he would rock Buck's head back and forth, whispering loving but pretend insult words like, "You're a stupid old dog, aren't you?" or "You're a lazy loafer."

Buck knew no greater happiness than when Thornton was doing that to him. And when his head was freed, Buck always had a smile on his face.

"You can almost speak, can't you Buck," Thornton used to say.

Buck had his own trick that showed his love for his new master. He would seize Thornton's hand in his mouth and gently bite it – not too hard.

"You're a lazy loafer."

Buck's love for Thornton was different from that of Skeet and Flash. If Skeet wanted love and attention, she just kept poking Thornton with her nose until he stroked her. Flash would just walk up and rest his head on Thornton's knee.

Buck normally kept his distance. There was a reason for that. Ever since Buck had first come to the north, none of his owners had stayed with him for very long. Each one had sold him on to another owner. He was afraid Thornton would do the same.

So Buck watched Thornton. He never let him out of his sight. He followed him around.

Yet, despite his great love for Thornton, Buck still had his newfound wildness and cunning. And now the wild was calling him. At first, it was a distant, half-heard cry that came from the forest.

Buck was sitting comfortably at the campfire one day when his ears suddenly perked up. He had heard a far off call and felt strongly drawn to it.

He ran into the forest and looked around. The call, whatever it was, could no longer be heard. Buck actually wondered why he had run into the forest.

His love for Thornton drew him back to the camp again.

It was as if there was a tug-of-war going on in Buck's heart. One part of him wanted to stay with Thornton. The other wanted to return to the wild.

A great urge to run wild and free with his ancestors seemed to be winning the battle.

Chapter 25
A Loyal Defender

Thornton's partners, Hans and Pete, eventually arrived with the raft. There was still ice about, but now the rivers were flowing fast. The journey to Dawson took no time at all.

Buck's love for Thornton continued to grow. There was nothing Buck wouldn't do for his new master. He obeyed and trusted him at all times.

One day, they moved on foot along the Tanana River. They camped on top of a cliff that evening. There was a large sheer drop to the rocks below.

Thornton was sitting right on the edge. He was in a playful mood and was joking about with Buck. Suddenly, he called to Hans and Pete who were sitting a little way off. "Watch this!"

The next moment he had raised his arm and pointed over the cliff edge. "Jump, Buck! Jump!"

Thornton was only joking. He was sure Buck

would stop at the edge. But Buck didn't hesitate. The dog was in mid-air when Thornton caught him. Another moment and Buck would have fallen to his death.

Buck almost falls to his death.

As it was, Buck almost took Thornton with him. Luckily, Hans and Pete rushed over and grabbed both man and dog.

"Unbelievable," said Pete, absolutely astonished. "That dog would have died for you."

"His loyalty is so strong," replied Thornton, "it worries me."

"I wouldn't want to be the man who attacked you with that dog around," said Pete.

A few months later, Thornton was in one of the gold towns having a drink in a bar. Buck was lying quietly in a corner. As usual, he had his head on his paws and was watching his master.

"Bad" Burton was an evil-tempered fellow, well known in that town for his violent behavior. He had a nasty habit of lashing out at people without any reason.

Thornton saw him walk into the bar and approach a young man, who was sitting quietly by himself and not doing anyone any harm.

Burton walked up to him and started arguing. The onlookers in the bar just stood and waited for Burton to hit him.

But Thornton decided to stop the argument then and there. He walked over and told Burton to calm down and go and have a drink.

Burton lashed out at Thornton without any

Buck knocks Burton to the floor

warning. Thornton was sent spinning and only saved himself from a nasty fall by hanging onto the bar.

Those who were watching suddenly heard something. It wasn't a bark or a yelp. It was more of a roar.

They saw Buck's body spring into the air as he left the floor on his way to Burton's throat. The man saved his life by throwing out his arm to defend himself.

The power of the attack knocked Burton to the floor. Buck landed on top of him with the man's arm clamped in his jaws. The man screamed and then Buck went for his throat again.

There was only one man who could save his life now and that was Thornton. He called Buck off.

Buck listened to his master, but he prowled up and down, growling furiously at Burton, who ran out of the bar.

The other people in the bar had no pity for Burton. It was his fault entirely. Burton had provoked the attack.

Several people were even brave enough to come and stroke Buck. He was a hero in their eyes. From that day on, his fame spread through every camp in Alaska.

Chapter 26
A Brave Rescue

Later on in the year, Buck saved John Thornton's life in another way. It happened when Thornton, Hans and Pete were trying to pull their boat across some dangerous rapids at Forty Mile Creek. This was where the smooth waters from upriver ran into an area of shallow rocks. The whole place was a cauldron of boiling and raging water.

Hans and Pete were walking along the bank with Skeet and Flash, hauling the boat with a thick rope. Thornton and Buck were on the boat.

There wasn't much pulling to do because the waters were so swift. Suddenly, the boat crashed into a rock under the water. Thornton was thrown into the air and landed in the river. The racing current swept him downriver towards the worst of the rapids.

Buck leapt from the boat and swam after his master.

He finally reached him and Thornton grabbed his tail. Buck swam towards the shore but the current was too strong. For every stroke Buck swam, the waters swept him and Thornton closer and closer to the rapids.

Thornton guessed Buck was losing the battle against the racing currents. He knew he had to let go or they would both drown.

He let go of Buck's tail when he saw a rock showing just above the surface. He got a slippery hold on it and held on for dear life. "Go, Buck! Go! Go!" he screamed above the sound of the roaring waters.

Buck was swept further downriver toward the boiling rapids. He looked back to his master. Thornton thought for one terrible moment that Buck was saying goodbye. But the dog struck out with his last remaining strength and reached the riverbank.

Thornton was now trapped in the middle of the river. Hans and Pete knew he wouldn't be able to hold on forever. But they had an idea. Hans hauled in the rope they had been using to pull the boat.

As soon as Buck returned, they tied one end of the rope to his collar. Hans and Pete held onto the other end.

Holding on for dear life

Buck didn't need to be told what to do. He leapt into the water and swam out towards Thornton.

The waters caught him again and swept him downstream. Hans and Pete pulled on the rope to help him back. Poor Buck had already broken some of his ribs in the struggle.

Now they tried again, this time starting a little higher up the river.

Buck, still with the rope around him, swam to a spot directly above Thornton. Then he let the current carry him down to his master. It worked. Thornton caught the rope.

Hans and Pete hauled the pair in. Both were dragged ashore almost unconscious. Thornton's dogs, Skeet and Flash, rushed over. Flash howled while Skeet played the nurse again. Buck woke up to find his face being licked.

The story of that day by the river became part of Klondike legend.

Though Thornton was bruised and battered, he went carefully over Buck's body. He found three broken ribs.

"That settles it," he said. "We camp right here."

They stayed until Buck's ribs had healed and he was able to travel again.

Skeet plays the nurse again.

Chapter 27
An Amazing Feat

During winter, Buck performed another famous exploit.

Thornton and Buck were in the Eldorado Saloon, at Dawson, when three gold miners walked in. They saw Buck sitting beside his master. They knew of his fame and couldn't resist boasting to Thornton that their dogs were better than Buck.

One of the men said that his dog could pull a sled with a five hundred pound load from a standing start. The second man boasted six hundred pounds for his dog. The last man, Matthewson, said his could pull seven hundred.

"Ha!" laughed Thornton, unable to resist the challenge. "Buck'll do a thousand."

"I'll bet a thousand dollars he can't," said Matthewson, slamming a sack of money on the bar. "There's my gold to prove it."

Nobody spoke. Thornton wished that he hadn't boasted about Buck's strength. In truth, he did not know if Buck could pull that weight. But he had great faith in the dog.

Matthewson added more pressure. "I've got a sled standing outside now. It's got twenty 50-pound sacks of flour on it now. That's a thousand pounds."

Thornton did not know what to do. The eyes of a dozen men were on him, silent and waiting. He didn't have a thousand dollars, nor had Hans or Pete. But O'Brien, the barman, was an old friend and Thornton asked him if he could lend him the money.

"Sure," said O'Brien, who had made a fortune in gold, "but I'm not certain Buck, or any dog, can pull a load that heavy from a standing start."

At that, the bar emptied. Everyone went into the street to see the contest.

***

Hundreds of people gathered to watch the challenge.

There was an argument to settle first. It was a brutally cold day with the temperature at close on sixty degrees below zero. The sled runners were frozen solid to the ground.

"I'll bet another six hundred dollars."

Some people said it was only fair that Thornton broke the hold of the ice before Buck started pulling. Others said that was Buck's job.

It was finally agreed that Buck would have to battle the ice as well as the thousand pound load.

Not one person in the crowd thought Buck could do it. Matthewson was sure he would win the wager. "I'll bet you another six hundred dollars on top of the thousand. What d'yer say?"

Thornton was getting worried. But his fighting spirit was aroused. The extra bet was on.

The men unhitched the team of dogs harnessed to the sled, which carried Matthewson's heavy load. Buck, wearing his own harness, was put in.

Buck had caught the mood of the moment. He knew that in some way he must do a great thing for Thornton that day. He was as excited as anyone.

The crowd greatly admired Buck. He was in perfect condition now. He was back to his normal weight and just about every ounce was muscle. In the chill wintry sun, his muscles rippled and his thick glossy coat gleamed.

But still no one thought Buck could pull a thousand pounds from a standing start.

Chapter 28
For the Love of a Man

The distance that Buck had to pull the sled was measured out. It would be a hundred paces. A pile of firewood marked the finishing line.

The crowd fell silent. Thornton kneeled down by Buck's side. He took his head in his hands and rested his chin on Buck's head. "If you love me, Buck. If you love me, Buck . . ."

That's all he said. Buck then took Thornton's hand between his jaws and made the gentlest of marks with his teeth. That was his reply.

Thornton stood up and stepped back. "Now, Buck, ready," he said.

Buck moved until the traces were tight. Then he moved back a step or so to give himself some slack. It was how he had learned to free a sled runner that was frozen to the ice.

"Gee! Gee!" cried Thornton.

Buck swung to the right. Then he jerked to the left, taking up the slack. The load shook. Everyone heard the sound of a crack.

"Haw! Haw!" shouted Thornton, encouraging Buck on.

Buck made the same movement, but this time to the left. There was another crack as at last the runners snapped free of the ice. Everyone held their breath. The tension was unbearable.

"Mush! Mush!" It was Thornton's final order.

Buck threw himself forward with a jarring lunge. The traces tightened and he pulled with all his might.

Buck's great chest was low to the ground; his head forward and down. His feet were scrambling, his claws cutting grooves in the hard-packed snow and ice.

The sled swayed, trembled and half-started forward. One of Buck's feet slipped. A man groaned aloud, as if it was all over. Then, the sled slowly lurched ahead in a succession of jerks.

The jerks turned into a smoother movement. The sled was moving faster!

Men gasped and started breathing again.

Thornton was running behind Buck, encouraging him at every step.

The crowd cheered as Buck moved closer and closer to the pile of firewood, which

Buck pulls with all his might.

Scherpenhuizen

marked the end of the hundred paces. The cheers turned into a roar as Buck reached the finishing line.

The crowd threw their hats into the air. Men shook hands. Thornton fell on his knees beside Buck and lovingly held his head in his hands.

"I'll give you a thousand dollars for him," yelled one of the spectators.

Thornton rose to his feet. The tears were streaming down his face. "No, sir," he said, "this dog is beyond price."

Buck affectionately took Thornton's hand in his mouth again. There never was a prouder dog than Buck that day.

Chapter 29
In Search of Gold

Buck earned John Thornton sixteen hundred dollars on that famous day in Dawson City.

Thornton used part of the money to take off on a trip with his partners in search of a fabled lost gold mine in the east of the territory.

The history of that mine was as old as the history of the Klondike. Many men had set off in search of the mine. More than a few had vanished forever.

It was said that one man had found gold and built a cabin nearby. Dying men had sworn to that story. They had also sworn that the nuggets found there were the finest ever seen.

But no man had ever seen the man or the gold. And the dead men were dead. So who was to know if any of that was true?

John Thornton wanted to solve the mystery. Along with Pete, Hans, Buck, Skeet and Flash, Thornton headed east.

They journeyed by sled seventy miles up the

frozen Yukon and swung left into the Stewart River. The ice was thick. It was easy traveling. They followed the river to where it began high up in the mountains.

John Thornton asked little of man or nature. He was unafraid of the wild. With a musket and a bag of salt for his food, he could live happily for as long as he wanted.

He was in no hurry. He hunted his dinner as he went. And if he failed to find food, he kept on moving. He knew that sooner or later he would find something to eat.

There was no need to carry great stores of food. The sled was loaded with ammunition, tools, buckets and pans.

To Buck, it was a journey of endless delight. He loved wandering through strange places he had never seen before. Sometimes, they would travel for weeks on end or camp for days at a time.

Sometimes they went hungry. Sometimes they feasted by a merry campfire, until they could eat no more.

Summer arrived again. They rafted across mountain lakes and raced down unknown rivers.

The months came and went, and back and

Feasting by a campfire

forth they journeyed in this vast country. No man had settled there yet, but they must have once, if the legend of the lost mine was true.

They journeyed through another winter. They did find a track once. But it started from nowhere and went nowhere.

Then they stumbled on an old cabin. Thornton walked up to a window and peered in.

Chapter 30
Gold!

John Thornton eagerly searched the cabin. In among some rotting blankets, he found an old rifle. But that was all. There was no clue to the men who had once hunted for beaver skins here.

And why on earth would anyone have left the gun behind? Perhaps he had never left. Perhaps he had died and been eaten by mountain beasts.

What they did find that morning was gold. They saw it glinting in a stream that ran close beside the cabin.

They were soon panning for nuggets. As Thornton, Hans and Pete scooped up earth from the bottom of the stream, the gold showed like yellow butter across the bottom of the washing-pans. Then, with a skilled hand, they used a circular movement to separate the gold from the dirt.

Gold was heavier than ordinary dirt. So, as

Searching the cabin

the dirt was washed away, the flecks of gold started to appear.

They spent many days panning for gold, picking up a fortune in nuggets and gold dust. They put the gold in sacks made from moose skins. They buried these beneath the cabin for safekeeping.

There was nothing much for the dogs to do. Occasionally, they had to carry back the animals that Thornton had shot for meat. Buck spent most of his time lying by the fire with Skeet and Flash.

And whenever Buck stared into the flames, he found his mind wandering back to that other world. He saw visions of that strange man again. Now, he too was staring into a fire.

Buck saw that the man seemed restless and scared of things moving about in the dark forest. He kept throwing more wood onto the fire.

Then Buck saw himself with that man in the forest. They were hunting together. The man could also spring up into the trees and swing from bough to bough. He never fell. He seemed as much at home in the trees as he did on the ground.

It was not just these pictures from another

Panning for gold

world that came to Buck. He also heard the call from the forest again.

It filled him with an uneasy, sweet gladness and wild yearnings. He felt drawn into the forest.

He would run through the scrub for hours sometimes. He especially liked to run in the dim, twilight world of midsummer when the light of the sun never vanished completely.

One night, he woke from a deep sleep. The call came to him from the forest. His nostrils quivered. His fur bristled. This time it was clearer than ever. It was a long drawn-out howl. Yet it was not the call of a husky dog.

The strangest thing of all was that this time he recognized it.

Buck sprang up. The howl was coming from somewhere much closer than before. He could hear it clearly.

He ran to a clearing in the forest. And there he saw a wonderful sight.

The man could swing from bough to bough.

Chapter 31
Buck's Wild Brother

What Buck saw was a long, lean, timber wolf. The young creature was sitting on its haunches on the edge of the clearing and howling. Its nose pointed to the sky.

Suddenly, the wolf stopped howling.

It turned towards Buck. For a moment they looked at each other. Buck prepared to be attacked. They circled each other. Then the wolf ran off. Buck gave chase.

The wolf was afraid of Buck. He was so much bigger. Yet somehow the wolf understood that Buck meant no harm.

At last, they stopped and faced each other. Buck sniffed the wolf. The wolf sniffed Buck. They became friendly. They played nervously.

The wolf started to walk away from the clearing. He did it in such a way as to show Buck that he must come with him.

Soon they were running side by side through the summer twilight, along a creek bed, through a gorge and up to the great mountain peaks.

They descended on the other side into a country of forest and stream. In the morning, they ran for hour after hour, while the sun rose higher and the day grew warmer.

Buck was happy in this wild, lonely land. He knew he was answering the call that had haunted him for so long.

They stopped by a running stream to drink. Then Buck remembered John Thornton. The wolf finished drinking and started off again. Buck was still torn by his love for Thornton. He turned around and set off for the camp.

The wolf turned and came back. For an hour, Buck's wild brother ran alongside him, whining and pleading for Buck to return and finish the journey. But Buck's heart was set on getting back to Thornton.

The wolf stopped and ran off alone. Soon after, Buck saw him on a hill. He was howling sadly towards the skies.

Thornton was eating dinner when Buck dashed into camp and sprang on him with great affection.

For two days and nights, Buck did not leave the camp and he never let Thornton out of his

Buck and the wolf sniff each other.

sight. He followed him about his work and watched him while he ate.

Then, Buck started to stay away from the camp for several days at a time. He crossed the mountains again and wandered for a week in the land of streams and forests.

He killed his meat as he went. He moved with an easy step and never seemed to tire. He hunted rabbits, beaver and other small creatures. He even fought and killed a large bear. He ate his fill, but when he returned two days later, he found a dozen wolves fighting over the remains. He scared them all away.

His longing for blood became stronger. He was now a hunter. A beast that lived alone in a place where only the strong survived.

He was bigger than most creatures in that land. His size and weight came from his father, the huge Saint Bernard. His jaw was a wolf's jaw, yet it was far bigger. His head was a wolf's, yet far broader. His cunning was wolf cunning and wild.

Buck was an all-powerful creature. No animal in the forest could match his strength.

Buck fights a large bear.

Chapter 32
Buck the Hunter

"I've never known a dog like Buck," said Thornton one day, as he watched Buck returning to the camp.

"There will never be another like him," agreed Pete.

"No, never," said Hans.

"I wonder where he goes," said Thornton.

"There's a wild streak in him," said Pete. 'I reckon there's a lot of wolf in him."

"The timber wolf is an ancestor of all dogs," said Thornton, "so it's not surprising if there's some wolf in him."

Thornton might have been surprised at the instant and terrible change in Buck whenever he reached the forest. He became the hunter again, a true animal of the wild.

When he hunted, he would crawl on his belly like a snake. He could catch a bird in its nest, or kill a rabbit as it slept. He fished for salmon in the stream, and caught them easily.

Fishing for salmon in the stream

Buck killed to eat, not for the pleasure of the hunt. He preferred to eat what he had killed for himself.

Summer passed again and the moose and the wild geese began their journey south. Buck had already killed a part-grown moose for food. He wanted a bigger beast to hunt down.

He came upon that animal one day up on the mountain. A band of some twenty moose had gathered. Their leader was a huge bull moose. It had a savage temper and stood over six feet from the ground. Buck could not have found a more difficult beast to face.

The bull saw Buck and roared in anger, galloping back and forth.

Buck used his cunning. He danced and barked in front of the bull until it chased after him. Buck was taunting the bull.

First he let it chase him, and then he hid. Next, he appeared from nowhere to worry the bull's cows. By the time the bull had come to their rescue, Buck was gone again. He would reappear to chase the young calves. This went on all day. The bull became angrier and angrier.

Then Buck started circling the bull. It snorted and scraped its hooves angrily in the

Buck attacks the moose.

dust, sometimes charging straight at Buck. The dog was far too quick for the bull.

This ceaseless taunting went on until twilight. By then, the bull was exhausted. He stood with his head lowered, watching the cows. He could not join them now. Buck, the merciless, fanged terror, stood in his way.

The moose was such a powerful beast. He had lived a long life and fathered many young. Yet now he faced death from a creature whose head did not reach above his knees.

From then on, night and day, Buck never left his prey. He never gave the beast a moment's rest. He threatened to attack whenever it tried to eat or drink.

The bull's head drooped more and more and its strength ebbed.

At last, at the end of the fourth day of his hunt, Buck attacked. His jaws caught the moose by the throat.

Buck stayed by the dead beast, eating and sleeping for a day and a night.

The next morning, Buck awoke with an uneasy feeling. Something had happened. He knew it. He had seen nothing and heard nothing. It was pure instinct.

He crossed back to Thornton's camp. The

nearer he got, the more he was aware that something terrible had happened.

The birds were talking about it. So were the squirrels. The very breeze whispered it.

Chapter 33
The Massacre

Buck followed the trail down the hill. His nose picked up more danger signals. The valley had fallen deadly quiet. Now, even the squirrels were silent.

As Buck slid along, his nose was jerked suddenly to one side by a new scent. He followed it into the bushes. He found Flash lying dead, with an arrow in his side.

Soon after, he found Hans. An arrow had killed him too.

Some distance further on, Buck heard singing. He picked up the echoes of a Yeehat chant. Buck looked down at the cabin and what he saw sent him into an overpowering rage.

He growled aloud with a terrible ferocity. For the last time in his life, he allowed his passion to come before his cunning.

And it was all because of his great love for John Thornton.

Some local Yeehat warriors were dancing

around the old cabin. They didn't hear Buck's growl. But they did see an animal bounding down on them at a frightening speed. They had never seen such a beast.

Buck hurled himself at them. The first man that Buck attacked was the chief of the Yeehats. Buck tore his throat out. The man next to him died before he even saw Buck hit him.

Flash is dead.

Buck rushed around like a mad dog. The Yeehats panicked and fled up the hill towards the forest. Buck, truly a raging fiend now, ran after them, snapping at their feet and dragging them down like moose. The Indians scattered far and wide.

When Buck returned to the camp, he found Pete dead by the campfire. He also saw the faithful Skeet lying dead by the pool close to the cabin. Buck knew that the loyal dog would never be far from its master. He was right. He found Thornton's body in the pool.

Buck felt a terrible loss. All day he brooded by the pool for the loss of Thornton.

Occasionally, he looked at the Yeehats he had killed. He felt a strange pride in what he had done. He had killed man, the noblest prey of all. And he had killed despite those men having clubs and bows and arrows.

The Yeehats had been no match for Buck. From that moment on, he would never be afraid of man again.

With John Thornton's death, Buck's last tie with man was broken.

Night fell and a full moon rose high over the trees into the sky. It lit the land with a ghostly white shroud. And with the coming of the

They had never seen such a beast.

night, Buck sensed life waking in the forest.

He heard a faint, sharp yelp. It was answered by other yelps echoing around the hills.

The yelps grew closer and louder. Buck put his nose in the air and sniffed. The wolves were coming.

Chapter 34
Battle of the Wolves

The yelping sound told Buck that the wolves had left their valley. Now, they were invading his.

Buck took up his position in the clearing by the cabin. He held his head high and puffed out his chest. As still as a statue, he watched them arrive.

The wolves poured into the clearing like a silvery flood beneath the moon. They stopped as soon as they saw Buck.

Most of the wolves stood in awe of Buck's size.

Not all were frightened. One leapt out of the pack and attacked Buck. In a flash, he struck back, breaking the wolf's neck.

Three other wolves tried to bring him down. Buck sent them running back into the pack.

The whole pack charged forward. Buck rose on his hind legs and snapped and clawed any wolf that came near him.

Still the wolves pushed forward. Buck gradually retreated. He was not worried because he knew what he was going to do.

Snarling and slashing, he kept the wolves at bay until he reached a spot that was protected on three sides by a high bank. Buck was safe now. All he had to do was fight the wolves in front of him.

And how he fought. The wolves battled him in turn. Not one could defeat him. They drew back at last.

One wolf, long and lean, approached Buck in a friendly manner.

Buck saw that it was his wild brother. It was the young wolf he had met before in the forest. He was whining softly. They touched noses.

Then, an old wolf came forward. He was thin and battle-scarred. Buck was ready to snarl. But the wolf was not going to attack. They sniffed each other.

The old wolf sat down in front of Buck, pointed his nose to the moon and started a long wolf howl. The rest of the pack sat down and howled.

Finally, Buck pointed his nose to the skies and howled.

Buck strode out of his corner and walked

A long wolf howl

among the wolves. They crowded around him, sniffing in a friendly way. Now they welcomed him as though he was one of the family. Indeed, he was.

The wolves started yelping in chorus. They continued yelping as they set off in the direction they had come. Buck went with them. He ran side by side with his wild brother.

Buck had joined the wolf pack.

Chapter 35
Ghost Dog

The years passed and Buck became the father of many wolf cubs in the wild.

The Yeehats saw something strange. They started seeing young wolves with a splash of brown in their gray coats. The change was inherited from Buck.

In years to come, they told of a ghost dog running at the head of the wolf pack.

They were afraid of that ghost dog because it was more cunning than they were. It stole from their camps, robbed their animal traps, killed their dogs and defied the bravest of their tribe.

The legend grew stronger. Hunters failed to return to camp and were later found dead. There were wolf footprints all around the bodies. But the prints were bigger than those of any known wolf.

Each fall, when the Yeehats hunted moose, there was a certain valley they never entered.

Running with the wolf pack

Ghost Dog

Scherpenhuizen

173

They thought of the spirits of men and of dogs in that valley. And now they thought that an evil spirit lived there.

Each summer there is one visitor to that great valley. It is a gloriously coated wolf-like beast. He is like, and yet unlike, all the other wolves.

He crosses alone into the clearing by the old cabin. There, he looks at the pool. The water once gleamed red with John Thornton's blood. Now it shines yellow from the gold still lying hidden in John Thornton's rotting moose-skin sacks.

Here, the visitor stops for a time and stares into the sky. He howls once – a long and sad howl for an old friend. Then, he leaves and returns to the wild.

On moonlit winter evenings, Buck can be seen running at the head of the wolf pack, a leader and a giant among wolves.

His throat bellows as he sings the song of the pack.

Buck has answered the call of the wild.

The End